For Karen Kondell and her wonderful family

*Many thanks to Rabbis Shira Milgrom and Bonnie Steinberg
for their generous guidance. Thanks also to my friend Carol Cott Gross,
who is always happy to advise, even when she is knee-deep in farfel.*
—S. S.

*For Marcia Wernick,
who has been known to perform miracles
from time to time*
—J. M.

it's a miracle!

A Hanukkah Storybook

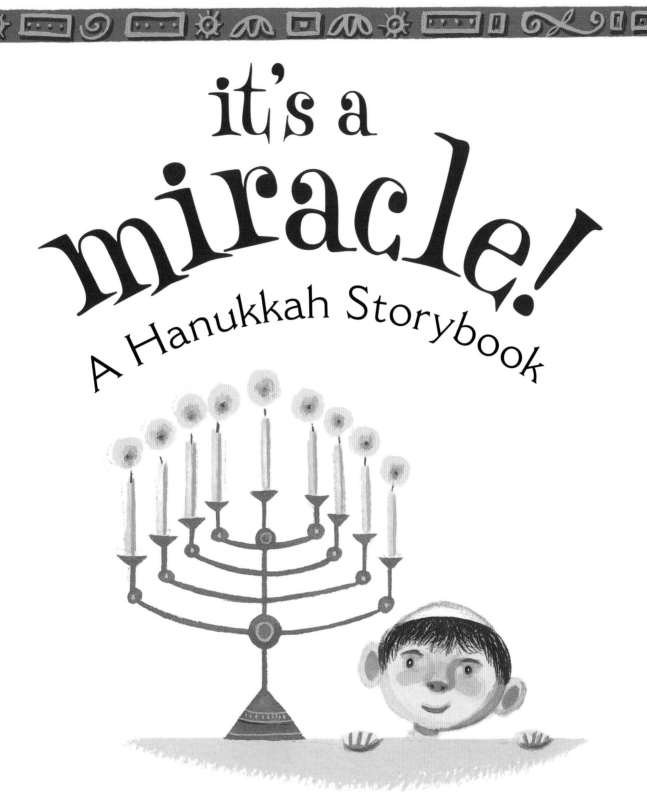

written by **stephanie spinner**   illustrated by **jill mcelmurry**

Aladdin Paperbacks

New York London Toronto Sydney

On the first night of Hanukkah, Owen Block ran down to the dining room two steps at a time. He was the new O.C.L.—the Official Candle Lighter— and he couldn't wait to start his job.

As the grown-ups sang the blessings, Owen lit the shammes, and then the first candle.

"Perfect," whispered Grandma Karen. "You're a natural!"

At bedtime she came to tuck Owen in. "Ready for a story?" she asked, sitting down and kicking off her shoes.

"Definitely," said Owen.

"Once there was a little girl who loved to light the Hanukkah candles," said Grandma Karen. "By the time she was three she knew all the blessings by heart, and she sang them perfectly while she and her brother lit the menorah."

"Wow," said Owen. He only knew *Baruch ata Adonai,* and he was six and a half.

"The girl's parents hoped their son would grow up to be a rabbi, but he wanted to study wolves, not religion, so he moved to Alaska.

"But their daughter couldn't get enough of the Torah. She liked reading it, she liked memorizing it, and she liked talking about it. By the time she was sixteen, she knew she wanted to be a rabbi. And even though it was unusual for a woman to be a rabbi in those days, that's just what she did."

"Like Cousin Shira?" asked Owen.

"Exactly like Cousin Shira," said Grandma Karen. Then she kissed Owen and turned off the light. "Good night, O.C.L.," she said.

"Good night, Grandma."

On the second night of Hanukkah, after Owen lit the candles, his mother served potato latkes.

"These are good!" said Owen's father. He sounded surprised.

Owen took a small bite. Usually his mother's latkes tasted like fried cardboard. But not tonight.

"Yum!" he said.

"New recipe?" asked Grandma Karen.

"I didn't change a thing," said Owen's mother, shaking her head. "It's a miracle!"

"Grandma, what's a miracle?" Owen asked later that night.

"Something unexpected and amazing," said his grandmother. "It can be a big thing, like the oil in the temple lasting for eight days—"

"That's the Hanukkah story," said Owen.

"Right you are," she said. "Or it can be a little thing, like making delicious latkes. Whatever it is, a miracle makes you glad to be alive."

She tucked him in, sat down, and kicked off her shoes. "Ready for a story?" she asked.

"Definitely," said Owen.

"Once there was a young woman who was expecting her first child. It was wartime, and her husband was fighting far away, so she went home to stay with her parents. They lived in Iowa."

"That's where Aunt Edna and Uncle Ralph live," said Owen. "Right?"

"Right," said his grandmother. "Anyway, after she had the baby she got very sick, and she had to stay in the hospital while her parents took the baby home. When she didn't get better, her parents sent a telegram to her husband, and he flew all the way to Iowa from France.

"The doctors told him that his wife might not live. Ralph wasn't a religious man, but then and there he started to pray. After a prayer or two he decided he needed help."

"Praying?" asked Owen.

"Yes. So he looked through the phone book and whenever he saw a Jewish name, he called the number. He told each person about his wife and asked them to pray for her. Everyone he called—I think there were five Jewish families in their little town—said they would. And you know what?"

"What?" said Owen.

"The very next day she started to get better."

"Really?" asked Owen.

"That's what I heard," said Grandma Karen. She kissed him.

"Good night, O.C.L.," she said.

"Good night, Grandma."

On the third night of Hanukkah, Owen's parents gave him a bag filled with gold coins.

"It's Hannukah *gelt*," said his father.

"It's chocolate," said his mother, showing him how to unwrap a coin. "See? You can eat it."

Not bad, thought Owen. And he ate it all up.

At bedtime Owen's grandmother came to tuck him in. "Ready for a story?" she asked.

"Definitely," said Owen.

"Once there was a little girl who wanted to be a cowgirl," she began. "Every day after school she put on her red cowboy boots and galloped around the house yelling, 'Giddy-up, bronco!' And every Hanukkah she asked her parents for a horse."

"Did she get one?" asked Owen.

"No," said Grandma Karen. "Her parents told her they didn't have room, not even in the garage."

"Did she cry?" asked Owen.

"No," said Grandma Karen. "She started saving up. She used her allowance for horse books and her baby-sitting money for riding lessons. After college she worked at the racetrack, cleaning stalls. Then she wrote a book about horses. It made her some money, so guess what she bought?"

"A horse!" shouted Owen.

"Bingo," said his grandmother. "A beautiful palomino, the exact color of matzoh."

"You had a horse, didn't you, Grandma?" asked Owen.

"I did," said his grandmother. "Her name was Lucky." She kissed Owen and turned off the light. "Good night, O.C.L.," she said.

"Good night, Grandma."

On the fourth night of Hanukkah, Owen's friend Buster came for a
sleepover. "Where's your Christmas tree?" he asked.

"We don't have one; we have a menorah," said Owen. "Want to help me
light it?"

"You're allowed to light matches?" asked Buster.

"Sure," said Owen. "At Hanukkah, anyway."

"Cool," said Buster. And they lit the menorah together.

At bedtime Owen's grandmother came to tuck them in. "Ready for a story,
boys?" she asked.

"Definitely," said Owen.

"Cool," said Buster.

"Once there was an alien who came to Earth by mistake," she began. "He was on his way to Mars, but he got off at the wrong stop, and he landed in New Jersey. At first he was so scared and confused that he couldn't remember who he was or where he was going.

"Then the alien saw a menorah in a window. It was the fourth night of Hanukkah, and a little girl had just finished lighting the candles. When the alien saw the menorah, he thought of his home planet, which had four shiny moons. And just like that, his memory came back.

"So right away he signaled the spaceship. It turned around and picked him up from the driveway."

"How come nobody saw?" asked Buster.

"Good question," said Grandma Karen. "The spaceship was lit up, but so was the neighborhood. There were lights everywhere shining and winking and blinking—menorahs, Christmas trees, icicles, Santas, reindeer—some even brighter than the spaceship. So nobody noticed it."

"Did you make that story up?" asked Owen.

"Maybe I did," said Grandma Karen. "And maybe I didn't."

She tucked the boys in and turned off the light.

"Good night, you guys," she said.

"Good night," said Owen and Buster.

On the fifth night of Hanukkah some wax burned Owen's hand while he was lighting the candles. But he didn't cry, and he didn't drop the shammes.

At bedtime Owen's grandmother came to tuck him in. "Is your hand okay?" she asked, sitting down and kicking off her shoes.

"Definitely," said Owen. "And I'm ready for my story."

"Once there was a boy whose parents cried all the time," Grandma Karen began. "The father was a pickle man and the mother was a chicken plucker, and they were very gloomy people. Their son kept getting sent home from school, which made them even gloomier."

"Was he bad?" asked Owen.

"No, he was the class clown," said Grandma Karen. "He caused so much commotion that the teacher—her name was Mrs. Pester—finally called his parents in.

"Mrs. Pester complained and complained, and when she was done his parents marched the boy home and sat him down at the kitchen table.

"'From now on,' said his father, 'you will behave yourself in school! Understand?'

"'Yes, Poppa,' said the boy.

"'From now on,' said his mother, 'you will do your clowning at home! Understand?'

"'Yes, Mama,' said the boy.

"'Start now!' said his father.

"'Now?'

"'Now!' said his mother. 'We want to see what all the fuss is about.'

"So the boy got up, and he belched the Alphabet Song with his eyes crossed. Then he blew grape juice out of his nose, and cartwheeled off the sofa.

"His parents gave him a big round of applause.

"The next day the boy juggled a sour tomato, three pickles, and a knish. And you know what?" asked Grandma Karen.

"What?" asked Owen.

"The more he clowned for his parents, the less gloomy they got. Once or twice they even smiled."

"What happened to the boy?" asked Owen.

"He grew up to be a comedian, with his own TV show."

"Like Uncle Izzie?" asked Owen.

"Exactly like Uncle Izzie," said his grandmother. She kissed him and turned off the light. "Good night, O.C.L.," she said.

"Good night, Grandma."

On the sixth night of Hanukkah, Owen's cousin Molly and her parents came to dinner. Molly helped Owen light the menorah, and then she gave him a big wooden dreidel. They spun it over and over again while the grown-ups drank coffee.

At bedtime Owen's grandmother came to tuck him in. "Ready for a story?" she asked.

"Definitely," said Owen.

"Once there was a dentist who loved his work," she began.

"Like Grandpa Harold?" asked Owen.

"Exactly like Grandpa Harold," said Grandma Karen. "Anyway, this dentist loved the smell of mouthwash in the morning. He said it was like perfume. He loved the drilling, and the filling, and the pointy little instruments lined up neatly on his tray."

"Eww," said Owen.

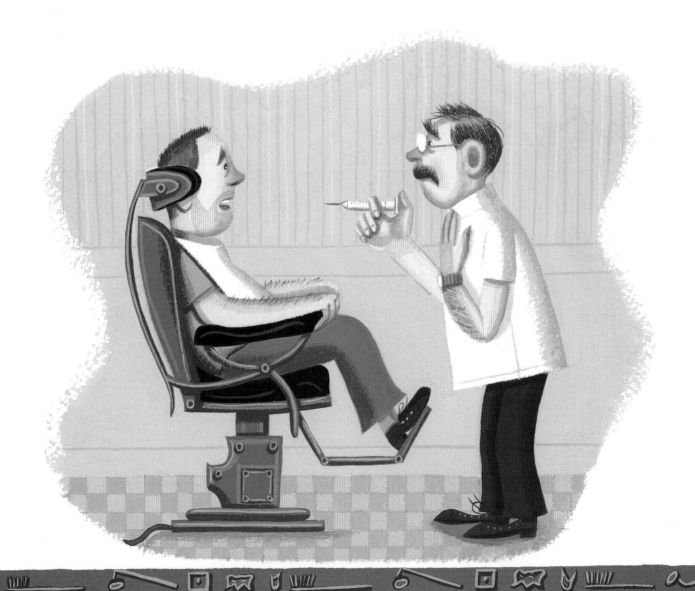

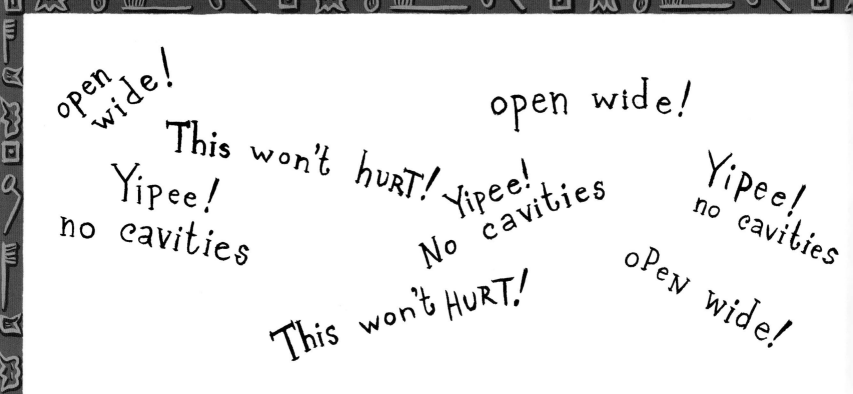

"The only thing he didn't like," said Grandma Karen, "was hurting his patients.

"Now this dentist had a parrot at home, a big funny bird with long toenails. The parrot's name was Dreidel, and all it said was 'Good yontif.' Do you know what that means?"

"'Good holiday'?" said Owen.

"Right you are," said Grandma Karen. "Anyway, Dreidel was so bored that he spent his time making snoring noises and pulling out his tail feathers.

"So the dentist taught Dreidel to say 'Open wide!' and 'This won't hurt!' and 'Yippee! No cavities!' Then he brought him to the office. And guess what?" asked Grandma Karen.

"What?" asked Owen.

Open wide!

Yipee!
No cavities

This won't HuRT

Open wide!

Yipee!
No cavities

This won't hurt

Yipee!
No cavities

"When the patients heard Dreidel, they forgot to be scared. As for Dreidel, he turned into quite an entertainer. By the time he retired, he knew how to sing the Dreidel Song.

"Oh dreidel, dreidel, dreidel, I made it out of clay," sang Owen's grandmother. "And when it's dry and ready, then dreidel I shall play . . ."

But Owen was fast asleep.

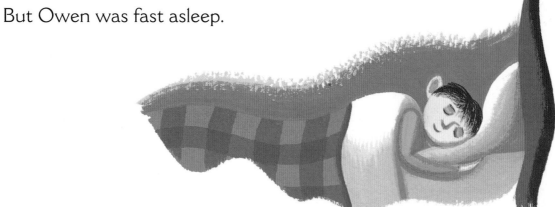

On the seventh night of Hanukkah, Owen sang the blessings while he lit the candles. He got most of the words right.

"Good job, sweetheart," said his grandmother.

"I'm impressed!" said his father.

"Me, too," said his mother.

At bedtime Owen's grandmother came to tuck him in. "Ready for a story?" she asked.

"Definitely," said Owen.

"Once there was a boy who wouldn't go to school," said Grandma Karen. "He told his parents he didn't want to grow up, he wanted to stay at home and play."

"What did they do?" asked Owen.

"They made a deal with him," said Grandma Karen. "They told him that if he went to school, he could be a baby when he came home. He could suck his thumb and play with his food and sit in his old high chair. He could even talk baby talk if he wanted to."

"Huh," said Owen.

"The boy did it for three months. Then, when Hanukkah rolled around, he decided he wanted to be the O.C.L."

"Babies can't do that," said Owen.

"Bingo," said Grandma Karen. "And the boy knew it. So he put away his baby stuff for good, and lit the menorah instead."

"What was his name?" asked Owen.

"Chip," said Grandma Karen.

"Like my father?!" asked Owen.

"Exactly like your father," said Grandma Karen. She kissed Owen and turned off the light. "Good night, O.C.L.," she said.

"Good night, Grandma."

On the eighth night of Hanukkah, Cousin Shira, Aunt Edna, Uncle Ralph, Grandpa Harold, and Uncle Izzie came for dinner. After Owen lit the candles on the menorah, everyone stood there for a moment, admiring its light.

Then they all sat down and ate a big meal.

"So, sweetie, I hear Grandma Karen's been telling you lots of stories," said Cousin Shira. "Did she tell you the one about the girl who wanted to be a rabbi?"

"Or about the dentist who had a parrot named Dreidel?" Grandpa Harold asked.

Owen looked back and forth between his two relatives. "Yes she did," he said.

"What about the
boy who juggled pickles?" asked
Uncle Izzie. "You know, he could wiggle
his ears before he could walk."

Owen nodded. "He could belch the Alphabet Song, too."

"He sure could," said Izzie, clearing his throat.

"Izzie—!" cried Grandma Karen.

"Did she tell you about the wife who was cured by prayers?" asked
Uncle Ralph. He reached for Aunt Edna's hand.

"Yes," said Owen. "She even told me about the girl with the palamino."

Grandma Karen smiled.

Owen looked around the table at all the familiar faces beaming at him.

"Okay, okay," he said, "I get it already!"

He grinned at his father. "Googly goo?" he asked.

"Googly goo yourself," said his father, and everybody laughed.

"Hey, wait a second," said Owen. "You don't expect me to believe there's an alien in the family, do you?"

"You never know, kid," said Uncle Izzie, wiggling his ears.

At bedtime Owen's grandmother came to tuck him in.

"Ready for a story?" she asked Owen.

"Definitely," he said.

"Once there was a boy who wanted to light the Hanukkah candles," she began. "And when he was almost seven, his parents finally let him. They made him the O.C.L.—the Official Candle Lighter—and he lit the menorah perfectly every night. And you know what?" asked Grandma Karen.

"What?"

"He did such a good job that they decided he should do it every year."

"Really?" said Owen.

"Definitely," said Grandma Karen. She kissed him and turned off the light.

"Good night, O.C.L.," she said. "And happy Hanukkah."

"Happy Hanukkah, Grandma," said Owen.

The Hanukkah Legend

Long, long ago, when Israel was known as Judea, a foreign king called Antiochus came to power. Other foreign kings had allowed the Jews to practice their religion in peace, but Antiochus was different. He wanted the Jews to pray to his gods, not their god, and when they refused, he punished them. He put statues of his gods in their temple, and decreed that Judaism was against the law.

Some Jews obeyed Antiochus. Others were defiant. They took refuge in the hills and came down to fight the king's army. Their leader was a great soldier named Judah Maccabee.

After three long years and many battles, these Jews finally succeeded in driving Antiochus and his army away. They returned to Jerusalem in triumph, eager to pray in their beloved temple. But a bitter surprise awaited them. The temple was in ruins, for Antiochus had allowed his soldiers to use it as they pleased.

Working day and night, the Jews repaired and cleaned the temple until it was spotless. All that remained was to bless it with pure oil. Then it would once again be a house of prayer.

Now the Jews met with another disappointment. They could find only one small jug of oil—hardly enough to keep the temple menorah burning for a day. But when they lit the oil, something mysterious and wonderful happened: The oil burned on for eight whole days and nights.

It was a miracle, and with it, the temple was sanctified.

The Jews rejoiced, giving heartfelt thanks to God. From that time on, they have celebrated Hanukkah for eight days—lighting the menorah, exchanging gifts, and remembering those who fought so bravely for the faith.

Hanukkah Blessings

First Blessing:

בָּרוּךְ אַתָּה יְיָ, אֱלֹהֵינוּ מֶלֶךְ הָעוֹלָם, אֲשֶׁר קִדְּשָׁנוּ
בְּמִצְוֹתָיו, וְצִוָּנוּ לְהַדְלִיק נֵר שֶׁל חֲנֻכָּה.

Blessed art Thou, Adonai our God, Ruler of the universe, who sanctified us with Thy mitzvot and commanded us to kindle the Hanukkah lights.

Baruch ata Adonai Eloheinu Melech ha'olam, asher kid'shanu b'mitzvotav v'tzivanu l'hadlik ner shel Hanukkah.

Second Blessing:

בָּרוּךְ אַתָּה יְיָ, אֱלֹהֵינוּ מֶלֶךְ הָעוֹלָם, שֶׁעָשָׂה נִסִּים לַאֲבוֹתֵינוּ
בַּיָּמִים הָהֵם בַּזְּמַן הַזֶּה.

Blessed art Thou, Adonai our God, Ruler of the universe, who performed miracles for our ancestors in days gone by, at this season of the year.

Baruch ata Adonai Eloheinu Melech ha'olam, she'asah nisim la'avoteinu bayamim hahem baz'man hazeh.

Third Blessing (said on the first night only):

בָּרוּךְ אַתָּה יְיָ, אֱלֹהֵינוּ מֶלֶךְ הָעוֹלָם, שֶׁהֶחֱיָנוּ וְקִיְּמָנוּ
וְהִגִּיעָנוּ לַזְּמַן הַזֶּה.

Blessed art Thou, Adonai our God, Ruler of the universe, who gave us life and sustained us, so that we might reach this season of the year.

Baruch ata Adonaoi Eloheinu Melech ha'olam, shehecheyanu, v'kiyemanu, v'higi'anu laz'man hazeh.

Glossary

Baruch ata Adonai (Hebrew): "Blessed art Thou, Our Ruler, Our God"; the opening phrase of many Jewish prayers.

Dreidel (Yiddish): a four-sided spinning top inscribed with the Hebrew characters *nun*, *gimel*, *hei*, and *shin*. They stand for the Hebrew words that mean "a great miracle happened there."

Gelt (Yiddish): gold; money.

Knish (Yiddish): a hefty, square-shaped, deep-fried snack, usually filled with potato.

Latkes (Yiddish): potato pancakes, traditional for Hanukkah.

Matzoh (Hebrew): large, flat Passover crackers symbolizing the unleavened bread the Jews carried with them as they fled from Egypt.

Menorah (Hebrew): a candelabra holding nine candles, one for each night of Hanukkah, and one for the shammes.

Mitzvot (Hebrew): commandments.

Sabbath: the day of rest. In Judaism, the Sabbath begins on Friday at sundown.

Shammes (Yiddish of the Hebrew word *shamash*): servant; in a menorah, the ninth candle, used to light all the others.

Torah (Hebrew): a written record of God's instructions to Moses, including the Ten Commandments; the basis of Judaism.

ALADDIN PAPERBACKS • An imprint of Simon & Schuster Children's Publishing Division • 1230 Avenue of the Americas, New York, NY 10020
Text copyright © 2003 by Stephanie Spinner • Illustrations copyright © 2003 by Jill McElmurry • All rights reserved, including the right of reproduction in whole or in part in any form.
ALADDIN PAPERBACKS and related logo are registered trademarks of Simon & Schuster, Inc. • Also available in an Atheneum Books for Young Readers hardcover edition.
Designed by Sonia Chaghatzbanian • The text of this book was set in Cantoria. • The illustrations for this book were rendered in gouache. • Manufactured in China
First Aladdin Paperbacks edition September 2007 • 2 4 6 8 10 9 7 5 3 1 • The Library of Congress has cataloged the hardcover edition as follows: • Spinner, Stephanie
It's A Miracle : a Hanukkah storybook / Stephanie Spinner ; illustrated by Jill McElmurry. p. cm. • "An Anne Schwartz book."
Summary: Every night of Hanukkah, Grandma tells a story at bedtime. Includes the Hanukkah legend. • ISBN-13: 978-0-689-84493-5 (hc.) • ISBN-10: 0-689-84493-X (hc.)
[1. Hanukkah—Fiction. 2. Grandmothers—Fiction.] I. McElmurry, Jill, ill. II. Title • PZ7.S7567 It 2003 • [E]—dc 21 • 2002006137
ISBN-13: 978-1-4169-5001-1 (pbk.) • ISBN-10: 1-4169-5001-X (pbk.)